I Don't Want To Go To Bed!

Tony Ross

Andersen Press
London

"Why do I have to go to bed when I'm not tired,
and get up when I am?" said the Little Princess.

Other Little Princess picture books

I Want My Potty
I Want My Dinner
I Want To Be
I Want A Sister
I Don't Want To Go To Hospital
I Want My Dummy
Wash Your Hands
I Want My Tooth

Little Princess Board Books are also available:
Shapes, Weather, Pets, Bedtime.
I Want My Potty, I Want My Dinner,
I Want To Be and *I Want A Sister*

Copyright © 2003 by Tony Ross
The rights of Tony Ross to be identified as the author and illustrator of this work
have been asserted by him in accordance with the Copyright, Designs and Patents Act, 1988.
First published in Great Britain in 2003 by Andersen Press Ltd, 20 Vauxhall Bridge Road,
London SW1V 2SA. Published in Australia by Random House Australia Pty.,
20 Alfred Street, Milsons Point, Sydney, NSW 2061. All rights reserved.
Colour separated in Switzerland by Photolitho AG, Zürich.
Printed and bound in Italy by Grafiche AZ, Verona.

10   9   8   7   6   5   4   3   2   1

British Library Cataloguing in Publication Data available.
ISBN 1 84270 223 8
This book has been printed on acid-free paper

"I don't WANT to go to bed!" she said.

"Bed is good for you," said the Doctor,
taking her upstairs. "Sleep is even better."

But the Little Princess came straight down again.
"I DON'T WANT TO GO TO BED!" she said.

"I WANT A GLASS OF WATER!"

"There you are," said the Queen.
"Sleepy, sleepy tighty."

"DAAAAAD!"

"You don't want another glass of water?" said the King.
"No," said the Little Princess. "Gilbert does."

"Nighty, nighty," said the King. "Sleepy tighty, Gilbert."
"Don't go!" said the Little Princess. "There's a monster
in the wardrobe."

"There's no such thing as monsters, and there are none in the wardrobe," said the King, closing the bedroom door.

"Dad!" shouted the Little Princess.
"What is it now?" said the King. "You're not still frightened of monsters?"

"Of course I'm not," said the Little Princess.
"Gilbert is. He says there's one under the bed."

"No, there isn't," said the King, creeping out
of the bedroom. "There are no such things."

"Stop her!" shouted the Queen. "She's escaped."
"I DON'T WANT TO GO TO BED!" said the Little Princess.
"Why?" said the Queen.

"There's a spider over my bed . . .
. . . and it's got hairy legs."

"Daddy's got hairy legs, and he's nice," said the Queen.

At last the Little Princess went to bed.

Later, when the King went in to kiss her
goodnight, her bed was empty.

Everybody hunted high . . .

. . . and low, until . .

"Here she is," said the Maid. "She's keeping Gilbert and the cat safe from spiders and monsters."

The next morning, the Little Princess got up
and yawned a yawn. "I'm tired," she said . . .

"I want to go to bed."